Oh ... Colours are nice! And I like numbers! 1, 2, 3, ...

Access – Allgemeine Ausgabe 2022
Band 1 – Let's go! – Einführungskurs für Lernende ohne Grundschulenglisch

Erarbeitet von der Englischredaktion
Filiz Bahsi (Konzept & verantwortliche Redakteurin),
Bonnie Glänzer, Graeme Garson (Redaktionsleiter),
Leon Ruland *sowie* Bea Herrmann

Lizenz- und Medienmanagement
Bettina Hamann

Illustrationen
Roland Beier, Berlin
Eva Muszynski, Berlin
Irina Zinner, Hamburg

Umschlaggestaltung und Layoutkonzept
Rosendahl, Berlin

Layout und technische Umsetzung
Compuscript Ireland and Chennai

www.cornelsen.de

Soweit in diesem Lehrwerk Personen fotografisch abgebildet sind und ihnen von der Redaktion fiktive Namen, Berufe, Dialoge und Ähnliches zugeordnet oder diese Personen in bestimmte Kontexte gesetzt werden, dienen diese Zuordnungen und Darstellungen ausschließlich der Veranschaulichung und dem besseren Verständnis des Buchinhaltes.

Dieses Werk berücksichtigt die Regeln der reformierten Rechtschreibung und Zeichensetzung.

Die Webseiten Dritter, deren Internetadressen in diesem Lehrwerk angegeben sind, wurden vor Drucklegung sorgfältig geprüft. Der Verlag übernimmt keine Gewähr für die Aktualität und den Inhalt dieser Seiten oder solcher, die mit ihnen verlinkt sind.

1. Auflage, 1. Druck 2024
Alle Drucke dieser Auflage sind inhaltlich unverändert und können im Unterricht nebeneinander verwendet werden.

© 2024 Cornelsen Verlag GmbH, Berlin

Das Werk und seine Teile sind urheberrechtlich geschützt. Jede Nutzung in anderen als den gesetzlich zugelassenen Fällen bedarf der vorherigen schriftlichen Einwilligung des Verlages. Hinweis zu §§ 60 a, 60 b UrhG: Weder das Werk noch seine Teile dürfen ohne eine solche Einwilligung an Schulen oder in Unterrichts- und Lehrmedien (§ 60 b Abs. 3 UrhG) vervielfältigt, insbesondere kopiert oder eingescannt, verbreitet oder in ein Netzwerk eingestellt oder sonst öffentlich zugänglich gemacht oder wiedergegeben werden.
Dies gilt auch für Intranets von Schulen und anderen Bildungseinrichtungen.

Druck: Athesiadruck GmbH
ISBN 978-3-06-03-4987-6

PEFC
PEFC/18-31-166
PEFC-zertifiziert
Dieses Produkt stammt aus nachhaltig bewirtschafteten Wäldern und kontrollierten Quellen
www.pefc.de

access 1

Let's go!
Einführungskurs für Lernende ohne Grundschulenglisch

Deinen Einführungskurs *Let's go!* findest du auch in der
Cornelsen Lernen App.

Siehst du eines dieser Symbole in deinem Einführungskurs, findest du in der App …

- alle **Audios**
- die Lösungen zu allen Aufgaben

Cornelsen

Write down English words you know.

Schreibe englische Wörter auf, die du kennst.

computer

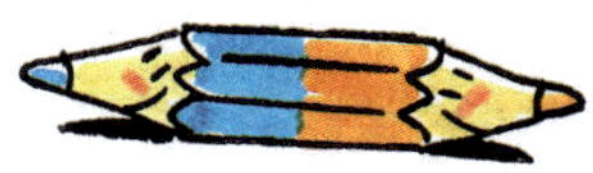

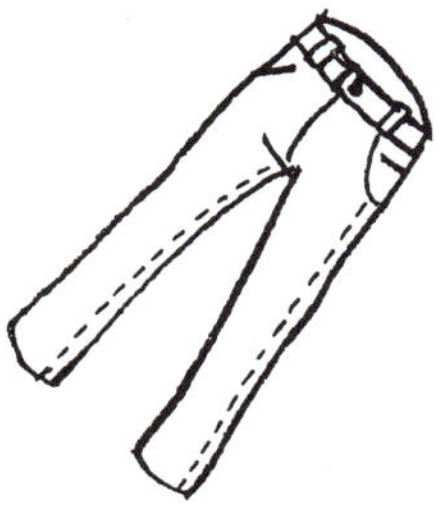

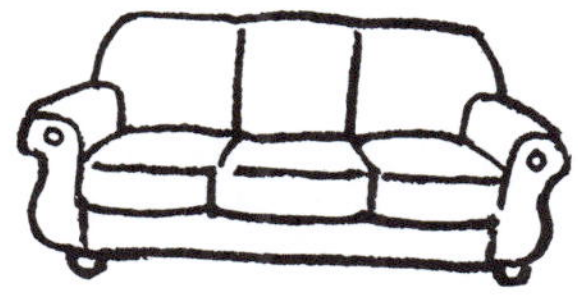

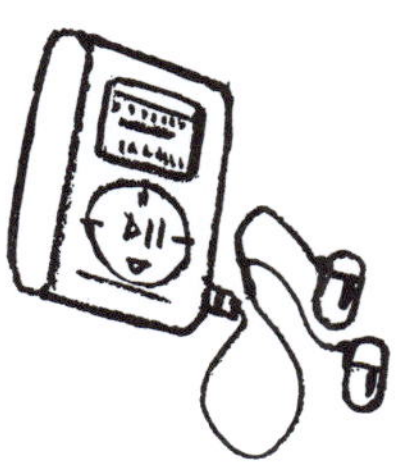

1 Hello, my name is ... Listen to the dialogue.

01

▶ SB (pp. 8–9)

Hallo, mein Name ist ... Höre dir den Dialog an.

2 Listen and read.

02

▶ SB (pp. 8–9)

Höre zu und lies mit.

Hello!
My name is Scout.
What's your name?

Oh, hi, er ...
My name is Parrot.

I'm eleven years old.
How old are you?

I'm ten
years old.

I'm from England.
Where are you from?

I'm from
England too.

What
about you?

I'm
- ◯ 9 (nine) years old.
- ◯ 10 (ten) years old.
- ◯ 11 (eleven) years old.
- ◯ 12 (twelve) years old.

I'm from ______________________________.

3 Look at the dialogue. Put it in the right order. Write numbers in the boxes.

Siehe dir den Dialog an. Bringe ihn in die richtige Reihenfolge. Schreibe Zahlen in die Kästchen.

► SB (pp. 8–9)

- [1] Hi.
- [ ] I'm from Brighton. Where are you from?
- [ ] I'm eleven years old. How old are you?
- [ ] I'm Alice. What's your name?

- [ ] I'm eleven too.
- [ ] I'm Zane. How old are you?
- [ ] Hello.
- [ ] I'm from Brighton too.

4 Now copy the dialogue from 3 in the correct order and practise it.

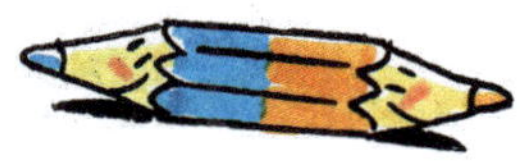

Schreibe nun den Dialog aus Aufgabe 3 in der richtigen Reihenfolge ab und übe ihn.

► SB (pp. 8–9)

______________________________ ______________________________

______________________________ ______________________________

______________________________ ______________________________

______________________________ ______________________________

______________________________ ______________________________

______________________________ ______________________________

______________________________ ______________________________

______________________________ ______________________________

5 Choose a boy or a girl from the pictures. Now you are this boy/girl. Use the information in the speech bubble and talk about yourself.

Wähle einen Jungen oder ein Mädchen aus den Bildern aus. Nun bist du dieser Junge / dieses Mädchen. Verwende die Informationen in der Sprechblase und stelle dich vor.

► SB (pp. 8–9)

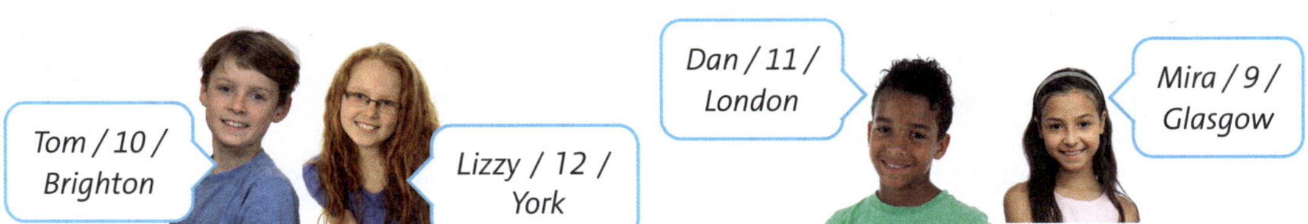

► Check

1 Find four colour words and colour them.

► SB (p. 10)

Finde vier Farbwörter und male sie aus.

gyellowreablobrowngranagpurpleblintepepinksplc

2 Write the colours. You don't need all the colours in the box.

Schreibe die Farben auf. Du brauchst nicht alle Farben im Kasten.

► SB (p. 10)

red • green • blue • pink • purple • orange • white • black • yellow • brown

3 What is yellow? What is blue? Listen, read and colour the pictures.

03

Was ist gelb? Was ist blau? Höre zu, lies und male die Bilder aus.

► SB (p. 10)

a yellow banana

green grass

a white snowman

red cherries

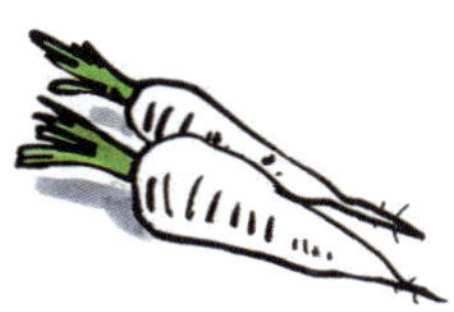

orange carrots

a blue swimming pool

brown cookies

a black piece of coal

a purple aubergine

a pink rose

► Check

4 What colours are the T-shirts? Listen and colour the T-shirts of the boys and girls.

04

Welche Farben haben die T-Shirts? Höre zu und male die T-Shirts der Jungen und Mädchen aus.

► SB (p. 10)

Fred ______

Jack ______

Kevin ______

Lisa ______

Lucy ______

Polly ______

Rick ______

Tim ______

5 Listen to the *Rainbow song* and sing along.

05

Höre dir den *Rainbow song* an und singe mit.

► SB (p. 10)

Red and yellow and pink and green, orange and purple and blue. I can sing a rainbow, sing a rainbow, sing a rainbow too.

6 Do a colour dictation. Tell your partner what colour to use for the numbers. Take turns.

Macht ein Farbdiktat. Sage deiner Partnerin / deinem Partner, welche Farbe sie / er für die Zahlen verwenden soll. Wechselt euch ab.

► SB (p. 10)

A

B

► Check

1 Say the chant and act it out.

Sage den Reim auf und spiele ihn mit Gesten vor. ► SB (p. 11)

2 Find the number words. Write them next to the correct numbers.

Finde die Zahlwörter. Schreibe sie neben die richtigen Zahlen. ► SB (p. 11)

E	T	N	B	F	V
I	W	I	S	I	X
G	O	N	E	V	U
H	S	E	V	E	V
T	H	R	E	E	W
Y	T	E	N	B	K
A	W	F	O	U	R

► Check

3 GAME: First choose nine numbers from *0* to *12*. Write them in the green boxes. Then say one number. Your partner has to write the number in one of the blue boxes. Take turns. At the end compare if you have the correct numbers of your partner.

SPIEL: Wähle zuerst neun Zahlen von *0* bis *12* aus. Schreibe sie in die grünen Kästchen. Sage danach immer eine Zahl auf Englisch. Deine Partnerin / Dein Partner schreibt die Zahl in eines der blauen Kästchen. Wechselt euch ab. Vergleicht am Ende, ob ihr die richtigen Zahlen der Partnerin / des Partners in die blauen Kästchen geschrieben habt. ► SB (p. 11)

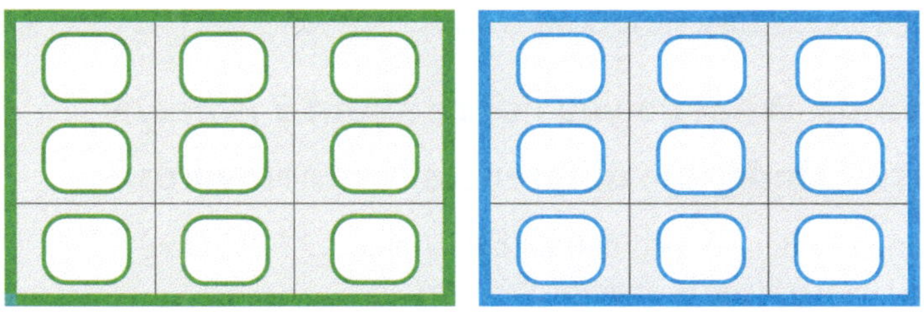

4 Harry and Amy are playing hopscotch. Write the number words in the boxes.

Harry und Amy spielen *Himmel und Hölle*. Schreibe die Zahlwörter in die Kästchen. ► SB (p. 11)

5 Listen and write the telephone numbers.

06

Höre zu und schreibe die Telefonnummern auf. ► SB (p. 11)

► Check

6 What's your telephone number? Write it down and tell it to a partner.

Wie lautet deine Telefonnummer? Schreibe sie auf und sage sie einem Partner / einer Partnerin. ▶ SB (p. 11)

1 My telephone number is ______________________________.

2 My partner's telephone number is ______________________________.

7 Do you remember the numbers up to *12*? Say them backwards.

Erinnerst du dich an die Zahlen bis *12*? Sage sie rückwärts auf. ▶ SB (p. 11)

8 Look at the number words. What do you notice about *3 (three)* - *13 (thirteen)* - *30 (thirty)*? Underline differences in other words.

Schaue dir die ausgeschriebenen Zahlen an. Was fällt dir bei *3 (three)* - *13 (thirteen)* - *30 (thirty)* auf? Unterstreiche Unterschiede in anderen Wörtern. ▶ SB (p. 11)

1	one	11	eleven	21	twenty-one
2	two	12	twelve	22	twenty-two
3	three	13	thirteen	30	thirty
4	four	14	fourteen	40	forty
5	five	15	fifteen	50	fifty
6	six	16	sixteen	60	sixty
7	seven	17	seventeen	70	seventy
8	eight	18	eighteen	80	eighty
9	nine	19	nineteen	90	ninety
10	ten	20	twenty	100	a hundred

9 Match and write the numbers.

Ordne zu und schreibe die Zahlen. ▶ SB (p. 11)

45	eighty
37	seventy-nine
79	eighteen
97	thirty-seven
80	ninety-seven
18	seventy-three
40	fifty-four
73	forty-five
54	forty

91 *ninety-one*

87 ______________________

55 ______________________

16 ______________________

64 ______________________

100 ______________________

43 ______________________

28 ______________________

99 ______________________

▶ Check

10 What number do you hear? Listen and circle the right number.

07

Welche Zahl hörst du? Höre zu und kreise die richtige Zahl ein.

► SB (p. 11)

1	13	31
2	15	51
3	12	20
4	8	18
5	17	77
6	34	43
7	25	52
8	40	14
9	76	67

11 Write the right number words under the numbers.

Schreibe die richtigen Zahlwörter unter die Zahlen.

► SB (p. 11)

36	54	63	88

12 Point at a number and say it. Take turns.

Zeige auf eine Zahl und sage sie. Wechselt euch ab.

► SB (p. 11)

► Check

1 Listen to the song *Seven days a week* and sing along.

08

Höre dir das Lied *Seven days a week* an und singe mit. ► SB (p. 14)

Monday, Monday! That's day one.
Go to school. Have lots of fun.

Tuesday, Tuesday! That's day two.
Here's a cookie – it's for you.

Wednesday, Thursday – three and four.
Come in please and close the door.

Friday! Five! It's time to go.
School is over now, you know.

Number six – that's Saturday.
We can stay at home and play.

Sunday, Sunday! Number seven!
Let's stay in bed until eleven.

2 Listen to the poem. Then finish it with the days from the boxes.

09

Höre dir das Gedicht an. Vervollständige es mit Wörtern aus den Kästchen. ► SB (p. 14)

Sunday · Saturday · Friday · Tuesday · Monday · Thursday · Wednesday

The days of the week

Day one of the week is ______________________.

Two ______________________, three ______________________, OK?

Then ______________________ and ______________________, and then: Hooray!

______________________, ______________________: we can play.

3 Read the poem in number 2 to a partner. Are the days right? Compare.

Lies das Gedicht in Aufgabe 2 einem Partner / einer Partnerin vor. Sind die Wochentage richtig? Vergleicht. ► SB (p. 14)

4 Listen to the poem again. Can you say it?

09

Höre dir das Gedicht noch einmal an. Kannst du es aufsagen? ► SB (p. 14)

► Check

5 Cover page 14. What day is it? Write the right word.

Decke Seite 14 ab. Welcher Tag ist es? Schreibe das richtige Wort auf. ► SB (p. 14)

1 NOMDAY ______ [1]

2 RUTHSDAY ______ [ ]

3 NUSDAY ______ [ ]

4 USTARDAY ______ [ ]

5 IRFDAY ______ [ ]

6 SUETDAY ______ [ ]

7 NEWSEDDAY ______ [ ]

6 Put the words in exercise 5 in the right order. Write the numbers of the days in the boxes.

Bringe die Wörter in Aufgabe 5 in die richtige Reihenfolge. Schreibe die Nummern der Tage in die Kästchen. ► SB (p. 14)

7 Complete the text. Write the correct day of the week.

Vervollständige den Text. Schreibe den richtigen Wochentag auf. ► SB (p. 14)

______ is between Monday and Wednesday.

Thursday comes before ______.

______ is day number 1 of the week.

______ is the last day of the week.

No school on ______.

______ is in the middle of the week.

8 What do you do on three days of the week? Write three days of the week and draw your activities.

Was machst du an drei Wochentagen? Schreibe drei Wochentage auf und zeichne, was du machst. ► SB (p. 14)

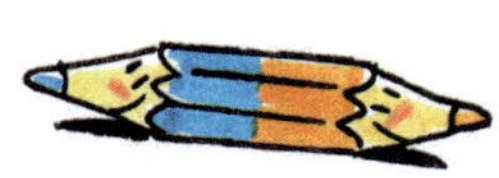

Monday ______ ______ ______

► Check

1 What's in the classroom? Listen and point.

10

Was ist im Klassenzimmer? Höre zu und zeige mit dem Finger darauf. ► SB (p. 14)

2 Which words are on the board? Circle and write them down.

Welche Wörter stehen an der Tafel? Kreise sie ein und schreibe sie auf. ► SB (p. 14)

✓ chair

3 What can you see in the classroom in number 2? Tick (✓) the words.

Was kannst du im Klassenzimmer in Nummer 2 sehen? Hake die Wörter ab. ► SB (p. 14)

► Check

4 Write sentences about your classroom.

Schreibe Sätze über dein Klassenzimmer. ▸ SB (p. 14)

board • chairs • desks • door • window	black • blue • green • orange • red • pink • white

1 In my classroom the *board is ...* ______________________.

2 In my classroom the ______________________.

3 In my classroom the ______________________.

4 In my classroom the ______________________.

5 In my classroom the ______________________.

5 Choose three pictures. Tell your partner what to do.

Wähle drei Bilder aus. Sage deinem Partner / deiner Partnerin, was er/sie machen soll. ▸ SB (p. 14)

Open the window.

Open your book.

Open the door.

Open your exercise book.

Close the window.

Close your book.

Close the door.

Close your exercise book.

▸ Check

1 What's in the schoolbag? Listen and tick (✓) the right answer.

11

Was ist in der Schultasche? Höre zu und mache bei der richtigen Antwort ein Häkchen. ▶ SB (p. 15)

1	☐ Alex	☐ Alex	☐ Alex	☐ Alex	☐ Alex
2	☐ Mike	☐ Mike	☐ Mike	☐ Mike	☐ Mike

2 Match and write down the words.

Ordne zu und schreibe die Wörter auf. ▶ SB (p. 15)

The green ruler is nice! What colour is your ruler?

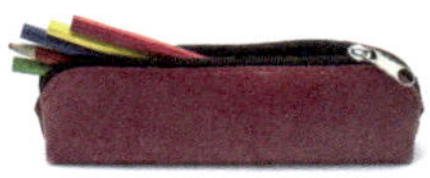

ru	case	______
school	ber	______
rub	ler	ruler
pencil	bag	______
pen	book	______
glue	cil	______
exercise	stick	______

▶ Check

3 This is Zane's schoolbag. Read his sentence. Draw and colour the school things.

Das ist Zanes Schultasche. Lies seinen Satz. Zeichne die Schulsachen und male sie aus. ► SB (p. 15)

I have a yellow ruler, a red rubber, a green pencil case, a pink book, five brown pencils, a black pen and two blue exercise books in my schoolbag.

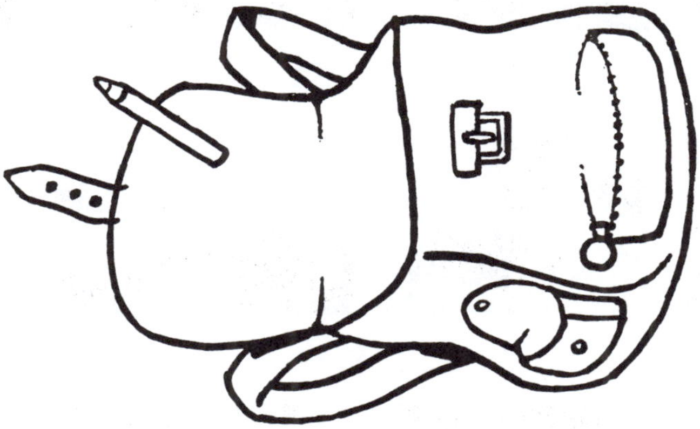

4 What's in Harry's pencil case? Write down the colours and the school things.

Was hat Harry in seinem Federmäppchen? Schreibe die Farben und Schulsachen auf. ► SB (p. 15)

Harry has an o *range* ______ p ______ ______.

In his pencil case he has a b ______ p ______,

a w ______ r ______,

a g ______ r ______,

______ r ______ p ______

and a p ______

g ______ ______.

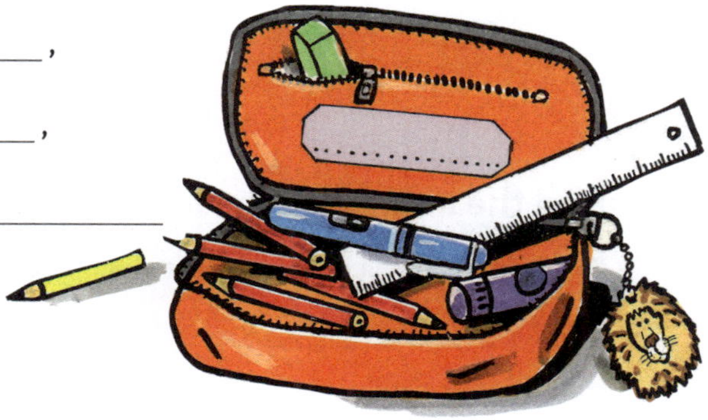

5 Listen to the song and sing along.

12

Höre dir das Lied an und singe mit. ► SB (p. 15)

► Check

1 Listen and look at the animals for one minute. Then close your book. How many animals can you and your partner remember? Say an animal name in English. Take turns.

13

▸ SB (p. 16)

Hört zu und seht euch die Tiere für eine Minute an. Dann schließt das Buch. An wie viele Tiere könnt ihr euch erinnern? Sagt jeweils einen Tiernamen auf Englisch. Wechselt euch ab.

1 
bird

2 
elephant

3 
lion

4 
horse

5 
monkey

6 
cat

7 
dog

8 
rabbit

9 
snake

10 
guinea pig

11 
bear

12 
rat

2 Find the animals in the letters. Underline them and write them down.

Finde die Tiere in den Buchstabenreihen. Unterstreiche sie und schreibe sie auf. ▸ SB (p. 16)

recath	*cat*	snakestdu	
tratx		schihorsepf	
sadogs		tomonkeyto	
meebeark		perabbitov	
birdcha		telephantion	
schlion		guguineatpigst	

▸ Check

3 Write the names of the animals in the puzzle.

Schreibe die Tiernamen in das Rätsel. ▶ SB (p. 16)

4 Do you have an animal at home? What is its name? Draw it. Or draw your favourite animal and give it a name.

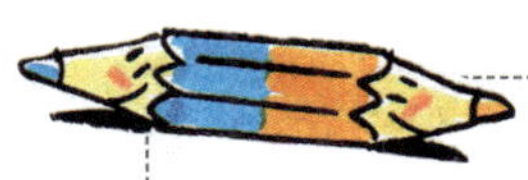

Hast du ein Tier zu Hause? Wie heißt es? Zeichne es. Oder zeichne dein Lieblingstier und gib ihm einen Namen. ▶ SB (p. 16)

I have a / My favourite animal is a ______________________.

Its name is ______________________________________.

▶ Check

1 Listen to the words for hobbies and look at the pictures. Read the words.

14

Höre dir die Wörter für Hobbys an und schaue dir die Bilder an. Lies die Wörter. ▶ SB (p. 17)

singing

dancing

music

swimming

basketball

rugby

running

football

computers

reading

films

photos

2 Find and write the hobby words.

Finde und schreibe die Hobby-Wörter auf. ▶ SB (p. 17)

1 mndrunningrrr ____________________

2 gahreadingbt ____________________

3 fghcomputerssgw ____________________

4 gfrmusickgl ____________________

▶ Check

3 Match and complete the sentences with the right hobbies. Draw lines.

Ordne zu und vervollständige die Sätze mit den richtigen Hobbys. Zeichne Linien. ▶ SB (p. 17)

1   I like ... dancing.

2   I like ... films.

3   I like ... reading.

4   I like ... singing.

5   I like ... computers.

4 What do you like? Write or draw two hobbies.

Was magst du? Schreibe oder zeichne zwei Hobbys. ▶ SB (p. 17)

1 I like ________________________________.

2 I like ________________________________.

▶ Check

1 This is me! Stick your photo here or draw a picture of yourself.

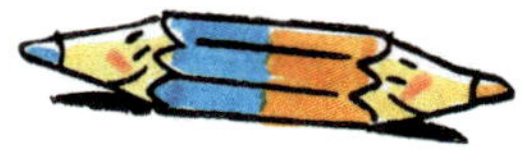

Das bin ich! Klebe hier ein Foto von dir ein oder male ein Bild von dir.

2 Write sentences about you.

Schreibe Sätze über dich.

My name is ______________________________.

I'm ______________________________ years old.

I'm from ______________________________.

My telephone number is ______________________________.

My English teacher is ______________________________.

I like ______________________________.

My favourite language is / My favourite languages are ______________________________.

My favourite animal is ______________________________.

My favourite book is ______________________________.

My favourite number is ______________________________.

My favourite song is ______________________________.

My favourite band is ______________________________.

▸ Check